CAJUN
Through and Through

by **Tynia Thomassie**

Illustrated by **Andrew Glass**

Little, Brown and Company

Boston New York London

For my brother Glen, the fisherman,
my brother Juan, the city boy,
and my cousins Jean and Jane,
who always keep me afloat

— T. T.

For David, Sarah, and William

— A.G.

First Edition

Library of Congress Cataloging-in-Publication Data

Thomassie, Tynia.
    Cajun through and through / by Tynia Thomassie ; illustrated by Andrew Glass. — 1st ed.
        p.   cm.
    Summary: Two boys who live in the bayou teach their prim city cousin how to be a true Cajun.
    ISBN 0-316-84189-7
    1. Cajuns — Juvenile fiction.   [1. Cajuns — Fiction.   2. Cousins — Fiction.   3. Louisiana —
Fiction.]   I. Glass, Andrew, ill.   II. Title.
PZ7.T36967Caj   2000
[E] — dc21   98-3662

10 9 8 7 6 5 4 3 2 1

SC

Printed in Hong Kong

The illustrations for this book were created with pencil, prepared medium,
and oil paint on star white paper.
The text was set in Latienne Medium, and the display type is Spumoni.

A Cajun Glossary and Pronunciation Guide

alligator gar
A fish common to the bayou that has a long snout like an alligator's

Baptiste
(bahp-TEEST)

Bayou Teche
(BY-yoo TESH) A bayou in Louisiana

Ça va?
(sah vah) French; short for *"Comment ça va?"* meaning "How's it going?"

crawfish boil
A festive party where crawfish are boiled in large quantities in big pots of highly seasoned water

fais do-do
(fay doh-doh) Literally means "make sleep" in French, but Cajuns use it to refer to a big party or dance. In the old days, one adult would be designated to watch all the sleeping children in a back room so that their parents could party and enjoy themselves late into the night.

gris-gris
(GREE-gree) A magic spell

gumbo
A delicious thick soup made from okra, spices, and seafood or chicken

How you makin'?
A Cajun abbreviation for "How are you makin' out?" (How are you doing?)

jambalaya
(JAHM-buh-LIE-uh) Another delicious Cajun dish, made from rice, sausage, chicken, and seafood all mixed together

mais
(may) French for *but*. Common in a Cajun phrase.

Maman
(mah-MAW^{n}) French for *Mom*

paddlebill
A very ugly fish common to the bottom of bayous

Remington Terrebonne Toups
(REM-ing-tun TEAR-uh-bone TOOPS)

Ti-Boy
(tee-BOY) *Ti* is short for the French *petit,* meaning little. (Ti-Boy is short.)

yaiiii
(yah-EEEE) A common Cajun whoop or cry of joy

outh of south, where the bayous bulge with alligators and cypress trees tickle the sky, two brothers, Ti-Boy and Baptiste, were passin' a good time.

Ti-Boy was hanging upside down from an oak branch, trying to stretch himself taller. And Baptiste was crackin' pecan shells and poppin' nuts into his brother's mouth. Those brothers were best friends, and they had no need of anyone else.

Just as Ti-Boy back-flipped off the branch,
a bell clanged.

"C'mon, Baptiste! Maman's callin' us!"

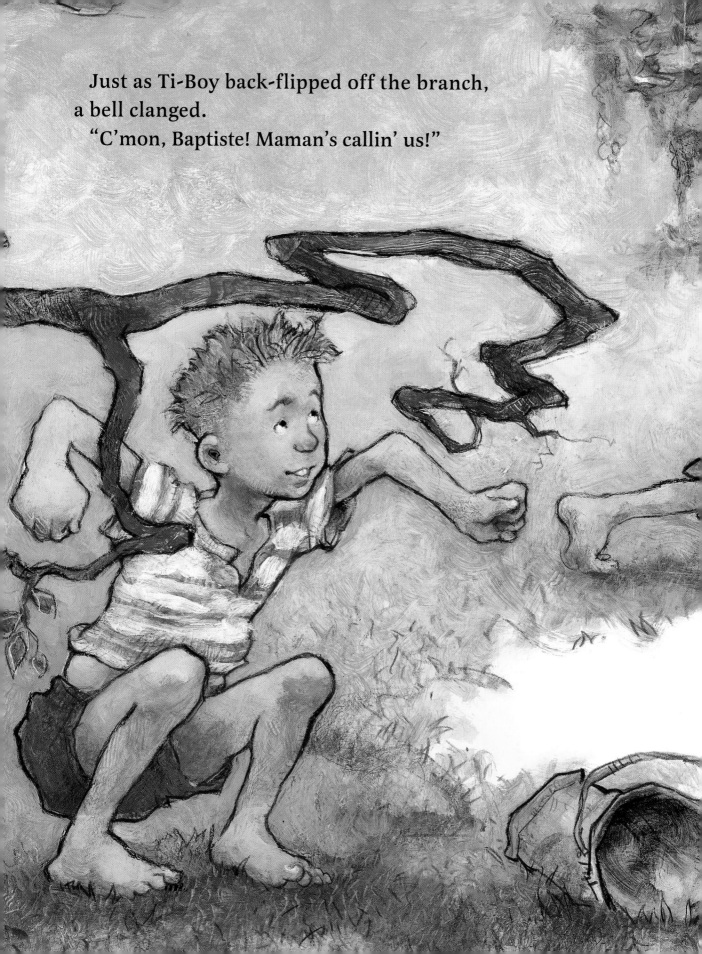

The boys raced each other back and crashed onto the porch as Maman clasped her hands and exclaimed, "Boys, I've got good news!"

"What, Maman? Is they gonna be a *fais do-do*?" asked Baptiste.

"A crawfish race?" asked Ti-Boy.

"Yo' cousin Remington's comin' from d'big city to visit fo' a spell," said Maman.

Hooo! You might as well have told them they were goin' to d'dentist to have teeth pulled, I'm a tol' y'all. Ti-Boy and Baptiste just shut their eyes, lettin' the nightmare sink in like old tires in fresh mud.

"Awww! Come on y'all!" Maman chided them. "Remington's family!"

Remington Terrebonne Toups was, at the very least, a good head scratch!

"Whoaver heard of a Cajun named Remington!" said Ti-Boy, shakin' his head.

"An' don't try to call him Remy, y'hear? It's REM-ING-TON," said Baptiste, imitating his annoyed cousin.

"It's a mouthful!" said Maman, chuckling. "But you two can show him a good time."

"Ohhh, Maman! 'Member d'last time he came down fo' a spell?" wailed Ti-Boy.

"He said d'gumbo was too rich an' d'jambalaya was too spicy!" declared Baptiste.

"He said a raw oyster looked like somethin' you coughed up after a bad cold!" topped Ti-Boy. "You wouldn't know he's a Cajun at all!"

"Boys, you jus' gotta be patient an' show 'im how t'ings get done here, dat's all," said Maman. "He really does wanna be yo' frien'."

Remington Terrebonne Toups arrived, carrying a small suitcase, sweatin' in the ninety-nine-degree heat in a coat and bow tie.

"*Ça va*, Remington?" greeted Baptiste.

"How you makin', Remington?" shouted Ti-Boy, slappin' him on the back.

"I'm not making anything," said Remington, a little confused. Ti-Boy and Baptiste just scratched their heads.

"Come out back, Remington," said Maman, taking off his coat. "D'family's all here, an' we're havin' a crawfish boil in yo' honor!"

Remington saw hundreds of little lobster-looking creatures heaped in a pile on the table outside. "How do you eat them?" he asked, looking a little queasy.

"You pull off d'heads, pinch d'tails, an' peel d'shell off like dis . . .
see?" In a blink, Ti-Boy unwrapped a crawfish tail and popped it
in his mouth.

"An' if ya *really* want a treat," Baptiste said with a wink, "suck
d'head!" Remington almost passed out.

Let's just say...the Cajun way of life was a little *different* for Remington. He tried his best to join in with Baptiste and Ti-Boy, but Remington felt like a shrimp out of water.

His cousins tried to start a spitting contest with watermelon seeds, but Remington wasn't game.

"Spitting's nasty," he said, wrinkling his nose.

They tried to take him swimming in Bayou Teche, but he wouldn't jump in the water.

"Why would you want to swim in water that's so...*brown*?" he said, backing away.

It was looking like they just couldn't find any common ground.

Maman walked in on the glum cousins and said, "Boys, why don't you take your cousin fishing an' catch me some dinner fo' tonight? I think he'd like that."

"Oh, Maman," said Ti-Boy, rolling his eyes, "Remington won't want to go fishin'! What's he gonna do when he has to bait his hook?"

Now, Remington realized that his cousins didn't think he had a great sense of adventure, but what self-respecting boy couldn't put a worm on a hook?

"I would love to go fishing," said Remington, with his head held high and his eyes staring straight ahead at no one in particular.

Ti-Boy and Baptiste chewed their lips while their eyes held conference. Then Ti-Boy said, "I *could* break in my new fishin' rod."

The boys motored out onto the bayou and sat in the scorching sun, but only *one* of them was havin' luck that day.

"Dang!" exclaimed Ti-Boy, holding up his fifth bass. "My new fishin' rod must have gris-gris on it, I'm catchin' so many fish!"

Baptiste couldn't believe *he* hadn't caught anything. But he knew how he'd even things up!

"Ti-Boy, be a good cousin an' let Remington have a go wit' yo' fishin' rod."

Ti-Boy shot Baptiste a look that could've stopped a chargin' bull.

"Oh, can I?" asked Remington, looking all pathetic. "I haven't even gotten a nip on *my* line." Now, Maman had raised her boys well, and you never said no to a guest — even if he *was* wantin' to try out your brand-new gris-gris deluxe fishin' rod. That wasn't the Cajun way!

"Don't get the line snagged," Ti-Boy cautioned. "I saved up fo' a whole year to get dat rod, so be careful."

No sooner had Ti-Boy spoken than Remington felt a tug on the line.

"Ya got somethin', Remington!" shouted Baptiste. "Set your hook! Set your hook!"

"Reel it in! Reel it in!" barked Ti-Boy.

Remington could see something dancing on the line, and he decided he was gonna get that fish, come heck or high water. But between shouts of "Hook, hook!" and "Reel, reel!" he could think of only one thing to do.

He stood up in the boat and threw the rod like a spear at the fish!

Mais, it's funny how a second can feel like a year, no? The three boys watched the fish and the fishing rod disappear in the water....Then all eyes fell on Remington. Ti-Boy — h'well, Ti-Boy couldn't *find* the words *he* would have liked to say. But his eyes said it all.

Remington knew his name was mud. He had to do the right thing — right away.

"Don't you worry, Ti-Boy," he said, ripping off his shirt and shorts. "I'll get it!" Before his brain could throw on the brakes, Remington took a big breath and dove into the brown bayou.

Somewhere, oh, between five and six strokes down, panic swept over Remington like a cold current of water. What am I *doing?* he thought. Will I even be able to *see* the fishing rod? I can hardly see one foot in front of me! Do I have enough breath? Will I bump into a snapping turtle? An alligator? These thoughts crossed his mind quickly, one tailin' the other, but his final thought was of Ti-Boy's glare, and he knew he had to keep going.

Each fish he passed was uglier than the next—paddlebill, perch, catfish, alligator gar. It was a good thing he *couldn't* really see what was keeping him company, cuz he would've fainted fo' sho! But Remington kept telling himself, I can *do* it, I can *do* it! I'm Remington Terrebonne Toups, and…I'm a Cajun, too!

Now, Ti-Boy and Baptiste were sitting in the boat, so dumb-founded that they were slow to kick into gear. "I can't believe he jumped in d'water," said Baptiste. "D'*brown* water!"

"H'man, if dis don't beat all!" exclaimed Ti-Boy with disgust. "My new rod gone, an' now we gotta go in after Remington."

Ti-Boy and Baptiste both cast off their shoes and shirts and dove in the bayou to find their cousin.

For a second, everything was still atop the water. Only a fat bullfrog, sunning himself on a nearby log, could appreciate what happened next!

Remington's head popped up, and he drank in a huge gulp of air.

Baptiste's head bobbed up, and he shouted, "Remington! You're all right!"

Ti-Boy's head broke above the water just as Remington lifted his right hand in the air.

"My fishin' rod! You found my fishin' rod!"

Then Remington pulled his left hand from the water, holding a wriggling fish, and shouted, "An' I got the bass, too!"

Yaiiii! Those boys laughed and splashed and carried on!

As they motored back home in the boat, Remington explained how he saw the rod glisten in the mud and saved it hook, line, and bass! But by the time the boys got home, the story kind of took on a life of its own, and to hear Ti-Boy and Baptiste tell it to Maman and Papa, Remington practically pulled that rod out of Moby-Dick's teeth!

"That's not exactly the way it happened," whispered Remington, beaming with pride as he ate his fried bass.

"Shoo', Remington," said Ti-Boy, chuckling. "You gotta tell the story the Cajun way — wit' a li'l spice!"

Baptiste raised his glass of root beer and cheered, "To our cousin, Remington Terrebonne Toups!" And as the family clinked glasses, Ti-Boy added, "A Cajun, t'rough and t'rough!"